S0-BYF-178

What a Treasure!

Families Reading Together

Palm Beach County
LIBRARY System
www.pbclibrary.org
Connect. Inspire. Enrich.

DISCARDED:
OUTDATED, REDUNDANT
MATERIAL

I Like to Read® books, created by award-winning
picture book artists as well as talented newcomers,
instill confidence and the joy of reading in new readers.

We want to hear every new reader say, "I like to read!"

_____

Visit our website for flash cards, activities, and more about the series:
www.holidayhouse.com/ILiketoRead
#ILTR

This book has been tested by an educational expert
and determined to be a guided reading level G.

What a Treasure!

I Like to Read®

HOLIDAY HOUSE • NEW YORK

I LIKE TO READ is a registered trademark of Holiday House Publishing, Inc.

Text copyright © 2006 by Jane Hillenbrand
Illustrations copyright © 2006 by Will Hillenbrand
All Rights Reserved
HOLIDAY HOUSE is registered in the U.S. Patent and Trademark Office.
The illustrations were done in egg tempera, oil pastel, and ink on canvas.
Printed and bound in November 2017 at Toppan Leefung, DongGuan City, China.
www.holidayhouse.com
5 7 9 10 8 6 4

Library of Congress Cataloging-in-Publication Data
Hillenbrand, Jane.
What a treasure! / by Jane Hillenbrand; illustrated by Will Hillenbrand. — 1st ed.
p. cm.
Summary: Mole digs with his new shovel, finding useful things
for the other animals and a new friend for himself.
ISBN 0-8234-1896-0 (hardcover)
[1. Moles (Animals)—Fiction. 2. Friendship—Fiction.
3. Animals—Fiction.] I. Hillenbrand, Will, ill. II. Title.
PZ7.H55772Wh 2006
[E]—dc22
2004060829

ISBN: 978-0-8234-3987-4 (ILTR paperback)
ISBN: 978-0-8234-3763-4 (board book)

To Ian—our inspiration and treasure
J. H. & W. H.

The day mole got his new shovel
he started to dig for treasure.

"Good luck," said his father.
"Have fun," said his mother.

"I bet you won't find
any treasures worth keeping,"
said his brother.

Mole dug.

He dug until he found a twig.

Bird flew down.

"Oh, what a treasure!" he chirped.

"It's just what I need
for a sturdy nest."

"Why don't you keep it?" said Mole,
and he began to dig some more.

Mole dug and dug.
He dug until he found a shell.

Snail crept over.
"Oh, what a treasure!" she exclaimed.

"It is just what I need
for a cozy house."

"Why don't you keep it?" said Mole,
and he began to dig some more.

Mole dug and dug and dug.
He dug until he found an acorn.

Squirrel scampered near.
"Oh, what a treasure!" he chattered.

"It is just what I need
for a delicious dinner."

"Why don't you keep it?" said Mole,
and he began to dig some more.

Mole dug and dug and dug and dug.

He dug until he found
another hole.

"Oh, what a treasure!" Mole shouted
as up popped a little mole.

"You are just what I need and want . . .

. . . a friend!"

"What luck!" said his father.
"How fun!" said his mother.

"I bet you'll want to keep this treasure," said his brother.

"Of course, why not?" asked Mole.

"Of course," answered
Mole's new friend.

Then Mole and his friend began
to dig some more.

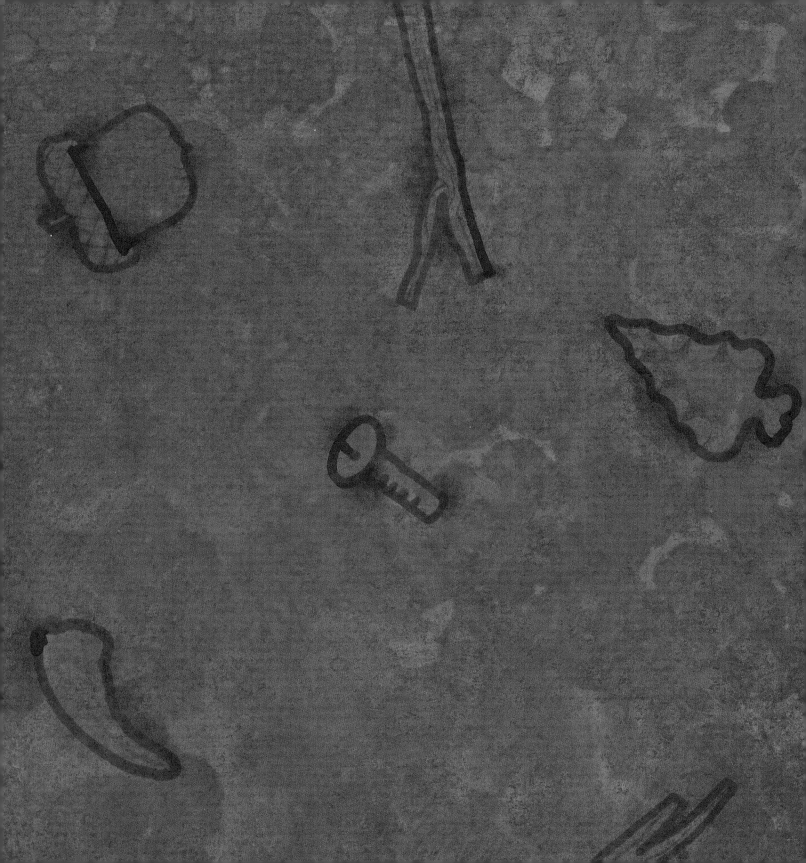